Rose

Olivia

Luther

scarlett

Lily

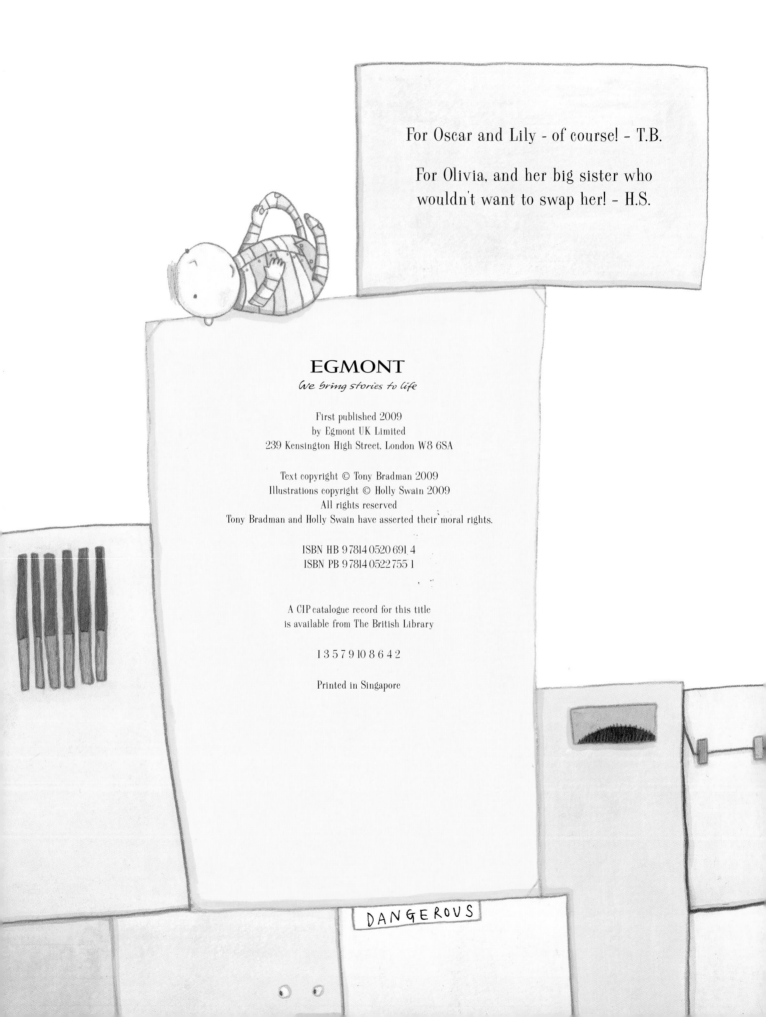

For Oscar and Lily - of course! - T.B.

For Olivia, and her big sister who
wouldn't want to swap her! - H.S.

**EGMONT**
*We bring stories to life*

First published 2009
by Egmont UK Limited
239 Kensington High Street, London W8 6SA

ISBN HB 978 1 4052 0 691 4
ISBN PB 978 1 4052 2755 1

A CIP catalogue record for this title
is available from The British Library

1 3 5 7 9 10 8 6 4 2

Printed in Singapore

DANGEROUS

# The Perfect Baby

By
Tony
Bradman

Illustrated
by
Holly
Swain

EGMONT

DRIBBLER

UATIC

When Lucy's parents brought her new baby
brother home from the hospital, they were
very,

    very,

        excited.

Lucy, however, was not impressed.

Baby William - for that was the baby's name - didn't really do all that much.
And what he did do was rather irritating.

He slept.

He woke up and cried.
He was fed.

He made some disgusting noises and smells.

And then he went
to sleep again.

'Well, what do you think, Lucy?' said her parents.

'I think . . . we should take him back to the hospital,' she said.

'Do you?' said her parents. Lucy could see that they looked a little disappointed. But they didn't argue.

So they all got in the car and headed for the hospital.

When they arrived, they went to the New Baby Department and rang the bell.

'Hi there!' said The Doctor. 'How may I help you?'

'Er . . . we want to return this baby,' said Lucy.

'No problem!' said The Doctor. 'Like to try another?'

'Well,' said Lucy, uncertainly. 'I don't know . . .'

'Please, Lucy!' said her parents. 'Please say yes!'
Lucy sighed, and gave in. 'Oh, all right then.'

NEW BABY DEPARTMENT

The Doctor grinned,
and gave them a tiny box.
'See how you get on with
this one,' he said.

And off they went.

As soon as they got home, Lucy's parents opened the box.
And inside was . . .

. . . a baby tortoise!

It was certainly different from Baby William.
It didn't cry. It didn't make disgusting noises or smells.
It poked out its little head and nibbled at some lettuce.
Then it went to sleep.

'Well, what do you think?' said Lucy's parents after a while.
'I think . . . we should take this one back, too,' said Lucy.

So they all got in the car and headed to the hospital.

'Back so soon?' said The Doctor. 'How may I help you this time?'

'Er . . . we want to return this baby,' said Lucy. 'It's too boring.'

'Really?' said The Doctor.
'But I take it you'd like another?'

Lucy's parents were
looking at her longingly.
Lucy sighed and gave in.

'Oh, all right then.'

The Doctor grinned, and gave them
a bigger box.
'Third time lucky, eh?' he said.

And off they went.

As soon as they got home, Lucy's parents opened the box.
And inside was ... a baby baboon!
It was certainly different from Baby William.

It didn't cry. It SCREEECHED very loudly.
It made amazingly disgusting noises and smells.

It swung from the lampshade. It broke things.

'Well, what do you think?'
said Lucy's parents after a while.
'I think . . . this one should definitely
go back,' said Lucy.

So they all got in the car and headed to the hospital.

oh my!

'**You again!**' said The Doctor.
'**Don't tell me. You want to return
the baby. What's wrong with it?
I can't believe this one was boring.**'
'Er . . . no,' said Lucy. 'It was
a bit too lively.'

'**I see,**' said The Doctor.
'**Fancy another try?**'
Lucy knew what her
parents would say.
She sighed and gave in.
'Oh, all right then.'

174532A

The Doctor grinned and gave them
a box that was a strange shape.
**_Fingers crossed, eh?_** he said.

And off they went.

As soon as they got home, Lucy's parents opened the box.
And inside was . . . a baby elephant!
It was certainly different from Baby William.
But it wasn't right either.

It was too

Soon they were back at the
hospital, swapping the elephant
for another baby.

shoo go away

That one was too **long. . .**

. . . and the one after that had too many legs.

PUT ME DOWN!

The one after that was way too

**tall . . .**

. . . and the one after that was too **hairy.**

look at all these tangles!

And the one after **that** was simply far too . . .

... SCARY!

So they all got in the car and headed to the hospital.

'Right, I give up!' said The Doctor.

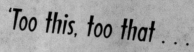

'Too this, too that . . .

you're just too fussy!'

Lucy's parents wailed.

But Lucy was thinking
about all the babies.

COME ON!

One hadn't been too boring,
  or too lively,
  or too big,
  or too anything.


'Excuse me,' said Lucy at last.
'If we have to have a baby ...
... we'll take the first one again, please.'


*'I don't know ...'* said The Doctor.
*'I'm not even sure where I put him.'*

Lucy frowned.

'Er. . . *just kidding!*' said The Doctor,
handing Baby William over.
'*Good choice!*' he said.
'*Bye . . . don't come back!*'

And off they went.

At home, Lucy's parents were very,

very,

excited.

And Lucy soon realised Baby William wasn't as irritating as those other babies.

He still didn't do very much.
But between the sleeping

WAAAAAA

and the crying

and the disgusting
noises and smells,

sometimes Baby William
was ... quite nice.

'Well, what do you think?' said Lucy's parents after a while.
'I think ...' said Lucy, and her parents held their breath.

'He's perfect.'

And he was . . . as far as babies go, anyway!